LEGENDS OF LONG AGO

LEGENDS OF LONG AGO

("Sieben Legenden")

By
GOTTFRIED KELLER

Translated by
CHARLES HART HANDSCHIN

Short Story Index Reprint Series

 BOOKS FOR LIBRARIES PRESS
FREEPORT, NEW YORK

First Published 1911
Reprinted 1971

INTERNATIONAL STANDARD BOOK NUMBER:
0-8369-3982-4

LIBRARY OF CONGRESS CATALOG CARD NUMBER:
71-167456

PRINTED IN THE UNITED STATES OF AMERICA

FOREWORD

GOTTFRIED KELLER, "the master-novelist of this age and without question its most original literary personality," was called by Paul Heyse "the Shakespeare of the short-story."

It is little wonder that the beauty and naïve atmosphere of his native city, Zürich, where he was born in 1819, should have inspired the art-loving lad to become a painter. Poor in worldly goods, bereft of a father at five, the lad fought and suffered bravely. After leaving school, he was apprenticed in succession to two minor painters of Zürich, and at the age of twenty-one went to Munich to continue his studies. But he was in financial straits most of the two years spent there, and his forte seems to have been fencing and rapier-fighting rather than art. In the fall of 1842, he returned home and took to literature.

Like Lincoln, he was no favorite with women. His first love was characteristic. In 1847, he fell a victim to the charms of pretty Louise Rieter, and was unhappy all summer because, poor and without a calling, he dared not importune her. Finally, one day in the fall, he wrote her a letter confessing his love but warning her against reciprocating it. He never married, but his pure regard for woman made him one of the foremost painters of feminine character known to modern literature.

.   .   .   .

We next find him in study at the University of Heidelberg, where he resolves to devote himself to literature. In Berlin, whither he next went, to gain a knowledge of the stage, he had again to battle with grim want. His first book of poems, published in Zürich, had not been remunerative. His first novel now proved no more so. He was proud. He would not return home. He would not write to his loved mother before he had made a name for himself. He was lonely and forsaken. He knew not whence his next meal would come. Pessimism was peeping in at his windows. It was then that his thoughts turned lovingly to his beautiful homeland, and out of the depths of his soul he wrote the first volume of that cycle of immortal stories, "The People of Seldwyl." The battle was won. His innate goodness of heart, his sturdy view of life, had triumphed.

After returning to Zürich he was given the position of Secretary of the Canton, which he held for fifteen years. The first fruit of his new life is our present cycle of stories, modern versions of lives of saints, under the title "Sieben Legenden,"—one of the seven being here omitted.

Keller's fame, now fully established, was augmented by several series of short stories, which earned for him, at the hands of an eminent German literary historian, the appellation of "the Swiss Goethe," and which made his name a household word in German speaking countries.

. . . .

Keller's townspeople are still fond of showing the favorite haunts of the old poet, who died in 1890, and of telling anecdotes of his kindly humor and genial bluntness. And well may the people of Switzerland point to him with pride, for it was the Florentine day of their national art when two men whose names would have made famous any city in Christendom, Gottfried Keller and Arnold Bocklin, lived and wrought in a single Swiss town.

. . . .

The "Sieben Legenden" represents Keller at his best. Their naïve ingenuousness, poetic charm, and quaint humor have made these legends a favorite book among German-speaking peoples the world over. They are offered here, for the first time in English, in the hope that this little volume may add to the enjoyment of many who love the wholesome and the pure in literature.

CONTENTS

SISTER BEATRICE

OR THE VIRGIN AND THE NUN

*Oh that I had wings like a dove! for then I would fly
away, and be at rest.—Psalm 55,6*

A CLOISTER lay high up on a mountain-
side and its walls shone afar over the
surrounding country. Within it were
many women—some beautiful, some ill-favored, all
of whom served the Lord and the Holy Virgin according to a strict discipline.

The most beautiful of the sisters was Beatrice,
the sacristan of the cloister. Of queenly form, she
moved from choir to altar performing her duties.
She kept the sacristy in order, and at the break of
day and again when the shadows of evening began
to fall, she tolled the cloister bell.

But ever and again she turned her wistful eye
from the billowy blue of the sky upon the passing
gleam of weapons or listened to the huntsman's horn
from the neighboring wood and the joyous calls of
the men, and a great longing to see the world filled
her bosom.

When at last she was no longer able to restrain
the desire of her heart, she arose one moonlit night

in June, put strong shoes upon her feet, and, ready for departure, approached the altar. "I have served thee faithfully for many a year," thus spake she to the Virgin, "but take now these keys from my hands, for I am unable longer to repress the yearning of my heart."

Then laying her bunch of keys upon the altar, she left the cloister. Down through the solitude of the mountain-side she wended her way until she came to a crossing of the paths in a forest of oaks, where, unable to decide in which direction to turn, she seated herself on a stone bench by the curb of a moss-covered fountain, and there rested through the dewy night until the break of day.

Over the tree-tops now there shone the first rays of the morning sun, and they fell upon a splendid knight who came riding up, clad in armor, and all alone.

The nun's beautiful eyes rested full upon the manly figure, but she remained so quiet that the knight had not seen her but for the plashing of the spring, which, striking his ear, directed his eye thither.

Straightway he made for the spot, dismounted, and, allowing the steed to quench his thirst, greeted the nun reverently. He was a crusader returning home after a long absence, alone, for he had lost all of his companions.

But in spite of his reverential demeanor, his admiring eyes never wandered from the fair face of Beatrice, who in turn continued to look in wonder and delight at the warrior, for here, certainly before her she beheld a part of the world for which she had longed in secret. Then she looked down abashed.

The knight now asked whither she was bound and whether he might be of service to her. The sound of his voice recalled her to herself, she raised her eyes to his again, and, confessing all, told him of how she had flown from the cloister to see the world, and that already she was in great fear and knew not whither to turn.

The knight laughed a hearty laugh and offered to conduct her to a safe road, should she feel disposed to entrust herself to him. "My castle," he added, "is not more than a day's journey distant; there you may prepare yourself in safety for your advent into the great and beautiful world."

She made no answer, but allowed him without resistance to place her upon his charger. Thereupon he himself mounted, and, with the happy nun seated in front of him, they rode merrily away through the wood and meadow.

[9]

The knight took great pleasure in the company of the sweet nun, while she, too, seemed not averse to him, and soon found herself listening to words of love as eagerly as though she had never heard a cloister bell.

And thus it is only natural that they saw but little of the passing landscape, or the sunshine, and the fair eremite willingly closed her eyes upon all the great world for which she had longed, save only the bit of it now being borne along upon the back of the faithful steed.

And Wonnebold, the knight, scarcely thought of the castle of his ancestors until its towers flashed out before them in the moonlight. All about the castle was quiet, and still more quiet was it within, and nowhere was there a light to be seen.

Wonnebold's father and mother had died, and all the serving people had left, save an old castellan. He appeared, after loud knocking and much ado, with a lantern in his hand, and he nearly died with joy when he caught sight of Wonnebold, without the castle gate.

Despite his desolation and his years, the old man had kept the castle in habitable condition, so that on this evening all was ready for the home-coming knight and his bride.

On the following morning, Wonnebold unlocked the great family chests and Beatrice robed herself in rich garments and bedecked herself with jewels. And this very day Wonnebold made her his wife, and she became a noblewoman, without a peer at the hunts, the festivals and dances, as well as in the humble dwellings of the dependants, and in the baronial pew of the church.

With varying fortunes, the years passed by, and as twelve summers came and went, she bore her husband eight sons, who grew up like young stags.

When now the oldest numbered eighteen winters, Beatrice arose one night in autumn from her husband's side, carefully laid away all of her worldly attire in the selfsame chests from which they had been taken years ago, and locked them.

In her bare feet now she stole from one bed to another, kissing her eight sons in turn, and finally laying the keys down by the side of her sleeping husband, she bent over him and imprinted a kiss of farewell upon his lips.

And now it was but the work of a moment to cut off the long tresses and to don her nun's garb of dark color, which she had preserved, and arrayed thus, noiselessly to leave the castle and take her way amid the falling leaves and rushing wind of the autumn night towards the cloister she had deserted many years ago.

As she walked on, she counted the beads of her rosary and pondered on the life she had enjoyed.

Thus undaunted, she continued her pilgrimage until she stood once more before the cloister-gate. She knocked. The now aged gatekeeper opened, greeting her casually as though she had been absent but half an hour.

Beatrice passed by her and, entering the chapel, cast herself upon her knees before the altar of the Virgin, who thus addressed her: "Thou hast been gone long, my daughter. All these years have I performed thy service, but I am glad now that thou hast returned and canst take charge of the keys once more."

And the Virgin bent down and handed the keys to Beatrice, who was transported in joy and wonder over the great miracle. She entered at once upon her service, putting this and that in order, and when the bell tolled the noonday hour, she found her way once more to the dining-hall.

Many of the sisters had grown old, others had died, new ones had come, and a strange abbess sat at the head of the table. No one seemed to notice the changes that had come over Beatrice, who had now taken her old-time seat, for the Virgin had performed the service in the person of Beatrice herself.

Ten years passed by and in the cloister preparations were in progress for the celebration of a great festival. On this occasion, each nun had pledged herself to lay upon the altar of the Virgin her rarest offering.

And thus one embroidered a costly banner, another a covering for the altar, and a third a chasuble. One wrote a Latin hymn, and a second set it to music, while another ornamented a prayer-book with drawings. Whoever was not at all able to do a thing of this sort, sewed a new garment to serve as a gift for the Christmas-tide, while the cook, perhaps, baked a dish of cakes.

Beatrice alone, listless, and absorbed in memories, dreams of the past, had provided no offering.

When, therefore, on the festal day, she brought no gift whatever, her sister nuns were amazed and chided her, and thus it happened that she stood humbly a bit to one side in the flower-bedecked sanctuary, as the nuns, in festive procession, laid their tributes in turn upon the altar, to the tolling of bells and the burning of incense.

And now the sisters raised up their voices and sang to the sound of music, and, as they did so, there appeared, clattering down the highway, a hoary horseman and eight stately youths, full armored, well mounted and followed by eight squires, ahorse. It was Wonnebold taking his sons to join the army of the Emperor.

Attracted by the festive service within, they drew up to the cloister gate, dismounted, and entered to offer up a prayer to the Virgin.

Within the sanctuary, all were astounded at the spectacle of the iron-clad old man kneeling with eight youthful warriors, steel-clad and looking like so many armored angels. The sister-musicians became confused, and for a moment the music ceased altogether.

Beatrice recognized her sons and her husband. She uttered a cry, hastened towards them, and, making herself known to them, she told her secret, and told, too, of the great miracle that had been vouchsafed her.

Now all confessed that hers indeed had been the richest offering. And even as they spoke there appeared upon each young warrior's head, bowed in prayer, a garland of fresh oak leaves, the testimony and the sign manual of the Queen of the Heavens.

EUGENIA

*The woman shall not wear that which pertaineth
unto a man, neither shall a man put on woman's
garment: for all that do so are abomination unto
the Lord thy God.—Deuteronomy 22,5.*

WHEN women lose their instinct for
beauty, grace and femininity and seek
to excel in other realms, it often hap-
pens that they don man's attire, and thus equipped
start out to make a trial of life.

Even the early Christian legends tell of in-
stances of such desire, and more than one fair saint
of those days sought to emancipate herself from the
bonds of tradition and the conventions of society.

Eugenia, a high-bred Roman girl, offers a case
in point. Her masculine proclivities betrayed her
into an adventure which placed her in great embarrassment, from which she was able to extricate
herself only by taking refuge in the time-honored
resources of her sex.

She was the daughter of a highly respected Roman citizen who lived with his family in Alexandria, a city that fairly swarmed with philosophers
and scholars of all kinds. Eugenia was carefully
reared and educated, and so much did she profit by ·

her instruction that as soon as she had outgrown her short skirts, she was allowed to attend the schools of the philosophers, scholiasts and rhetoricians, like any male student. On the occasion of such visits, she had a bodyguard of two beautiful lads of her own age to accompany her, the sons of former slaves of her father, who were being educated with Eugenia and taking part in all of her studies.

She grew up the most beautiful maiden anywhere to be found, and her two companions, both of whom, strangely enough, were called Hyacinthus, also increased in stature and comeliness. Wherever Eugenia, the fair rose, appeared, there on her right and left, might be seen also the two Hyacinths rustling and gliding gracefully along a few steps behind her, their mistress carrying on a disputation with them over her shoulder as they walked.

Never had a fair blue-stocking two better trained associates. They never differed with their mistress and always allowed her to remain a step in advance in the acquisition of knowledge. Thus she always got the better of an argument and never stood in danger of saying anything more stupid than her companions.

All the bookworms of Alexandria composed odes and epigrams upon this favorite of the muses, and the complaisant Hyacinths had to copy these verses carefully upon golden tablets and carry them after their mistress.

With each semester she grew more lovely and learned, and already she was exploring the intricate maze of the Neoplatonic philosophy when the young proconsul, Aquilinus, conceived an ardent passion for her and asked her hand in marriage. Her father, however, felt so deep a respect for his daughter's learning that he waived his right as a Roman father to dispose of her hand, and, not presuming to urge her in the slightest, referred the suitor to the girl herself, though personally no man would have been more gratifying to him as a son-in-law than Aquilinus.

Eugenia herself had long been favorably impressed with Aquilinus, the stateliest, most respected, and courteous man in Alexandria, and one who, moreover, was considered to have a fine wit and a generous heart.

Nevertheless she received the devoted consul with perfect coldness and dignity, surrounded by rolls of parchment, the two Hyacinths standing behind her chair. One of these wore a robe of azure, the other, one of rose, while Eugenia herself was dressed in immaculate white. Thus a stranger might have been in doubt whether he had before him three fair, tender youths, or three blooming maidens.

Before this tribunal the worthy Aquilinus stepped, clad in a simple, dignified toga, anxious to give vent to his passionate emotion in tender and loving words. But when Eugenia showed no intent of dismissing her companions, he took a seat opposite her and broached his suit in few straightforward words, restraining himself meanwhile, for as he gazed enraptured upon her fair face and form, a great desire overcame him to cast himself at her feet.

A smile dimpled Eugenia's cheek, but she did not even as much as redden, so completely had her great learning and mental discipline checked all the finer feelings of her woman's heart. Assuming a serious and profound mien she answered him thus:

"Thy desire, O Aquilinus, to have me to wife does me great honor, but I cannot allow myself to be moved to a rash act thereby, for such it would be, if, without searching our hearts we should follow the promptings of the first impulse. The foremost quality that I should desire in my future husband is that he respect my scholarly endeavors and ambitions, and participate in them. And thus I should be pleased to have you come often to my house to emulate me and my companions in striving for the highest knowledge. In this way we should learn whether or not we are suited to each other, and after some time spent thus we may be able to understand each other as is becoming divinely created beings, who are called to walk not in darkness but in the light."

Not without a secret flush of anger, but with a proud dignity, Aquilinus replied to this pompous speech: "If I did not understand and appreciate you, Eugenia, I should not desire you to wife. As for me, I am known to every one in Rome as well as in this province. If, therefore, with all your learning you are not able at this time to recognize me for what I am, I fear you never will be. Nor am I here with the intention of becoming a schoolboy once more, but to take a wife. As for these two children, it would be my first desire, should you become my bride, that you dismiss them and return them to their parents, to whom they might be of some use. And now I pray you answer me not as a sage, but as a woman of flesh and blood."

At this, a flush of deepest carnation overspread the face and neck of the beautiful philosopher and with a heaving bosom she replied: "My answer, O Aquilinus, is ready, since I perceive from your words that you do not truly love me. At this I am not grieved but it does offend the daughter of a noble Roman to be lied to."

"I never lie," said Aquilinus sternly. "Farewell."

Eugenia turned away, and Aquilinus strode deliberately from the house. She was about to resume her studies as though nothing had happened but the written page became blurred before her eyes. She was unable to go on and asked the Hyacinths to read to her. But in vain; her blood was stirred and her thoughts were far away.

For if she had, up to this time, looked upon the consul as the only acceptable man among all of her suitors, should she decide to wed, now he had become to her a thorn in the flesh that allowed her neither peace nor rest.

Aquilinus continued quietly to perform his duties, reproaching, meanwhile, in secret, his own foolish heart which would not forget the pedantic beauty.

Nearly two years passed. Eugenia had become more and more a remarkable and brilliant personage, while the Hyacinths had grown to be two great louts whose chins showed the first symptoms of a beard. Although people now began to pass remarks about this unusual companionship, and instead of the complimentary epigrams of former days, satiric ones began to appear, Eugenia could not bring herself to dismiss her body-guard. It seemed imperative to retain it, for had not Aquilinus seriously objected to it?

Aquilinus, however, continued quietly on his course and seemed to give no further heed to her. Neither did he pay attentions to any other woman. He seemed no longer to think of marriage, and people began to find fault, saying so high an official ought not to remain unwed.

All the more stubbornly did Eugenia resolve not to give up her companions, who seemed so objectionable to him, for she was determined not to appear desirous of pleasing him. Moreover, she loved to do as she wished, in defiance of custom and public sentiment, and to preserve the consciousness of a pure life, under conditions which for other women might have been dangerous and even ruinous. Vagaries of this sort were quite common with women of that day and age.

But Eugenia was not happy. She had her

scholarly companions philosophise on heaven and earth and hell, only suddenly to interrupt them, in order that they might accompany her out into the fields for miles and miles, without even vouchsafing them a word.

One morning she decided to visit a near-by country-seat. She herself drove, and was in a charming mood. It was a clear spring day and the air was laden with the scent of balsam. The Hyacinths were basking in her good humor, and thus they passed through a suburb just as the Christians were holding their Sabbath services. From monastery and chapel there resounded divine song. Eugenia reined in her horse to listen, and heard the words of the psalm: "As the hart panteth after the water brooks, so panteth my soul after thee, O God. My soul thirsteth for God, for the living God."

At the sound of these words, coming as they did from pious, humble lips, her proud soul gave way, her heart was transfixed, and seemed suddenly to know exactly what it desired. Slowly, without speaking, she continued on the way to her country villa. Here she clothed herself in male attire, and, calling the Hyacinths, left the house, without having been seen by the servants.

She returned to the monastery, knocked at the

gate and introduced herself and her companions as young men who wished to be accepted into the monastery as monks; for, said she, "We desire to separate ourselves from the world and live for God." She was well schooled in theological lore and answered the questions the abbot put to them so well that he accepted the three of them into the cloister and had them invested with the monastic garb.

Eugenia became a handsome, almost angelic monk and was called Brother Eugenius. The Hyacinths were likewise, willingly or unwillingly, transformed into holy brothers, for they had not even as much as been asked whether they wished for the change, and had long ago become accustomed to live only by and through the wish of their feminine example and mistress. Still they took kindly to the monastic life, since they enjoyed more leisure than heretofore, were no longer obliged to study, and were able to give themselves up entirely to a passive form of obedience.

Brother Eugenius, on the other hand, did not grow lax in his zeal, and he became a renowned ecclesiastic, with a face white as marble but with glowing eyes and the port of an archangel. He was the means of converting many heathen; he cared for the sick and suffering, searched deeply into the Scriptures, preached in golden tones, clear as a bell, and upon the death of the abbot was chosen as his successor, thus becoming the superior of seventy monks, great and small.

Now when Eugenia and her companions had disappeared so mysteriously, and were nowhere to be found, her father inquired of an oracle what had become of his daughter, and learned in answer that she had been caught up by the gods and placed among the stars. Straightway the heathen priests heralded the event abroad in order to boast a miracle before the Christians, while the latter had in reality derived the good from it, and had, so to speak, the hare already in their kitchen. The heathen priests went further, and even designated a star, with two lesser satellites, in the heavens as the new constellation. The good people of Alexandria came out on the streets and the house-tops to peer into the heavens, and many a man who had formerly seen Eugenia on her walks, now revelled in the reminiscence of her beauty and fell in love with her as he gazed with tear-dimmed eyes upon the star that twinkled so serenely in the billowy vault.

Aquilinus, too, peered into the heavens, but he shook his head and failed to fall in with the conventional belief. All the more firmly, however, did the father of the deified girl believe in it. He took not a little pride in the fable, and with the aid of the priests had it decreed that a statue should be erected to her memory and divine honors be shown her. Aquilinus, from whom governmental permission to this end had to be obtained, gave it on condition that the statue be made in the very figure and image of the apotheosized girl. This was an easy matter, since there were extant a great number of busts and likenesses of her. A marble statue was accordingly erected in the outer court of the Temple of Minerva, a statue that the artist needed not to be ashamed of, since it was, in spite of its realism, ideal, and a work of art as to figure, posture and garments.

When this piece of news reached the cloister, the seventy monks were not a little put out over the card the heathen priests had played, in the erection of the new idol and the impious deification of a mortal woman.

Most of all did they have their fling at the woman herself, calling her a jade and a mountebank, and during the noonday hour they carried on an unusual noise and bustle. The Hyacinths, who had become good-natured little dominies and who bore the abbot's secret buried in their breasts, looked significantly at him. He, however, beckoned them to be quiet, and paid no heed to the noisy rant, tolerating it as a punishment for his former heathenish mode of life.

But the following night, Eugenia arose from her couch, and armed with a heavy hammer, left the cloister softly, to destroy the statue. She took her way to the marble-studded portion of the city, where the temples and public buildings stood, and where she had passed the years of her childhood.

Not a soul was astir in the quiet world of granite. As the girlish monk ascended the steps of the temple, the moon, rising over the shadows of the city, cast its silvery light upon the columns of the outer court. There Eugenia caught sight of her statue. White as the fallen snow, of wonderful grace and beauty, the delicate folds of the drapery hanging chastely about the shoulders, it stood, with fine spiritual expression, and lips ready to smile.

The Christian maiden approached curiously, with hammer raised in hand. As she surveyed the statue close by, a sweet thrill coursed through her soul. The hammer fell to the ground, and she gave herself up to the enjoyment of her former self in silence.

As she did so, a sense of bitter melancholy overcame her, a feeling as though she had been expelled from a beautiful world and were astray in the desert, a hapless shade. For though the statue was idealized, it expressed Eugenia's one-time true self all the more faithfully, the real self which her bookishness had only temporarily eclipsed. It was therefore not mere vanity that brought her to recognize her better self now in the magic moonlight, and that awakened in her the feeling that she had made a mistake.

Suddenly she heard the sound of a man's determined step, and involuntarily she concealed herself in the shade of a marble column, from where she saw the form of Aquilinus approaching. He walked up to the statue, gazed upon it long, and finally laying one arm about the girlish shoulders, softly pressed a kiss upon the marble lips. Thereupon wrapping himself in his toga he walked slowly away, looking back more than once, as he did so, upon the resplendent form of white.

Eugenia found herself trembling violently. Angry and excited, she strove to collect herself and with raised hammer stepped up to the statue to put an end to this idolatry forever. But instead of shattering the beautiful head, she burst into tears, and, like Aquilinus, she too pressed a kiss upon its lips. Then she hastened quickly away as she heard afar the step of the night-guard approaching.

With heaving breast she stole back to her cell. That long night, until the sun arose, she slept not, and during the matins, which she overslept, she dreamed of many things which had nothing whatever to do with morning prayers.

The monks, believing that their abbot needed sleep because of protracted spiritual vigils, allowed him to slumber on until at last they found it necessary to rouse him on account of a special emergency.

An aristocratic widow who was ill and in need of spiritual aid had sent word that she desired the ministration and advice of the abbot, Eugenius, for whose zeal and high personality she had long felt a deep reverence. The monks did not wish to allow so good an opportunity of enhancing the honor of the church to pass unheeded, and they therefore hastened to awake the abbot.

Half asleep and with flushed cheeks, as they had not seen her for many a day, she started on her way, her thoughts tarrying more with her morning dreams and the columns of the temple than on the business in hand.

Thus she entered the house of the heathen suppliant, was led to a chamber and left alone with her. A beautiful woman of less than thirty summers lay upon a couch, but, strange to say, looking not at all like an ill or contrite person, but aglow with the proud joy of life. Scarcely could she control her feelings until the supposed monk had, at her request, taken a seat by her bedside, when she seized both his white hands, pressed her forehead upon them and covered them with kisses.

Eugenia, who was occupied with her own thoughts, paid little heed to the passionate bearing of the woman, and regarding her actions as a token of humility and spiritual contrition, made no attempt to restrain her. Encouraged by this, the fair heathen threw her arms about Eugenia's neck.

Utterly dazed, Eugenia recovered from her absent-mindedness. At the same time the woman poured into the ears of the terrified monk a perfect torrent of words, confessing her love and seeking in all manner of ways to convince him that it was his duty to return it.

Eugenia gathered herself up in towering rage and set the pagan siren severely to rights, retorting with fearful imprecations, such as only a monk has at his command.

When the woman saw her plan foiled, she suddenly changed her tactics. Like a tigress she sprang towards Eugenia, raising so murderous a commotion that her maids rushed in from all directions.

"Help! Help! This man has assaulted me," she cried, suddenly releasing her hold on Eugenia, who arose breathless in confusion and fright. The maids took to screaming even more loudly than their mistress, and, running hither and thither, attracted male help by their cries. Eugenia was unable to speak a word for fear, and fled from the house filled with shame and disgust, pursued by the din and curses of the mad mob.

Nor did the malicious widow hesitate to go directly to the consul, Aquilinus, followed by a goodly retinue, there to accuse the monk of base misdemeanor. She told how he had in his hypocritical manner entered her house, first to importune her by attempting to convert her to the Christian faith, and, having failed in this, to assault her flagrantly.

Her entire retinue attested the truth of these assertions, whereupon Aquilinus had the cloister immediately surrounded by troops, and the abbot, with the monks, brought before him for trial.

"So this is the sort of work you carry on, is it?" he asked them in his severest tones. "Do you already feel your importance so much that you, whom we have barely come to tolerate, insult our women and go about like ravenous wolves? Did your Master, whom I honor more than you do, ye hypocrites,—did He teach you to do such deeds? You are a motley assemblage and a pack of rascals. Defend yourselves, if you can, against the accusation."

The shameless woman now repeated her story, which she punctuated with hypocritical sighs and tears. When she had finished and had again veiled herself with great propriety, the monks looked in fear at their abbot, whose virtue they never doubted, and raised up their voices to deny the false accusation.

On the other hand, not only the followers of the lying woman, but also a number of neighbors and passers-by who had seen the abbot flying from the house in shame and confusion, and who naturally believed him guilty, emphatically attested his guilt, thus silencing the poor monks by great odds.

The monks looked again upon their abbot, this time somewhat in doubt, reminding him that if he was guilty the punishment of God would speedily follow, just as they even now gave him over to worldly justice.

At this all eyes were directed upon Eugenia, who stood forsaken in the midst of the crowd. She had been found weeping in her cell when she was taken into custody along with the monks, and during the entire trial had stood with eyes downcast, her cowl drawn far down over her face. She was in a serious predicament. If she preserved the secret of her identity and her sex, she fell a victim to the false accusation. If she disclosed it, she would bring down a greater storm of disapproval and certain ruin upon the cloister, for a monastery that had as its abbot a beautiful young woman could not escape unfortunate suspicion and ridicule at the hands of the evil-disposed heathen round about.

Now, this fear and hesitation would not have agitated her had she still been, according to monastic notion, of an undivided heart. But since the past night, doubt had entered her soul, and the meeting with the wicked woman had only served to confuse her still more. She had not, consequently, the courage to take a decided stand and bring about a miraculous solution.

But when Aquilinus requested her to speak, she

remembered his former affection for her, and trusting to this, bethought herself of a way of escape. In soft and gentle tones she pleaded not guilty to the charge and offered to prove her innocence to the consul, if he would grant her a private audience.

Something in the tone of her voice moved Aquilinus. He granted her the desired interview, had her taken to his residence, and was closeted there with her alone.

Eugenia raised her eyes to his, threw back her cowl and said: "I am Eugenia, whom thou once didst desire to wife."

He recognized her at once and was convinced that it was she. At the same time a great storm of wrath and jealousy arose in his bosom at the thought that his old love had lived for so long a time among a company of monks.

He restrained himself, and while eyeing her with close scrutiny feigned disbelief in her words, saying: "You do indeed look very much like that erratic girl. But what is that to me? What I want to know is about your affair with this widow."

Eugenia now related the entire story, timidly and anxiously. From the manner of her recital, Aquilinus saw at once the falsehood and the base-

ness of the accusation. Nevertheless, he replied
with apparent calmness: "And if you are Eugenia,
as you say, how did you become a monk, how was
it possible, and what was your object in so doing?"

At these words she blushed deeply and cast
down her eyes in embarrassment. And still it
seemed not unpleasant to her to be there and to
be able to converse with a good old friend concerning herself and her past life. Without hesitation
she related simply and sincerely all that had happened to her since her disappearance, taking good
care, however, not even so much as to mention the
two Hyacinths.

Her story pleased him not a little, and moreover, it was becoming more difficult for him with
every passing moment to conceal his joy at finding
his long-lost love. But he controlled his feelings
and resolved to learn from her conduct in this
whole affair whether she was still the modest and
chaste Eugenia of former days.

With this object in view he said: "Your story
is a very good one, yet I consider the girl whom
you allege you are incapable of such escapades,
despite her former caprices. The true Eugenia
would at least have preferred to become a nun.
Why in the world should a woman, no matter how

learned and pious she might be, desire to don a monk's cowl and live with a company of seventy monks?   And so I shall continue to consider you a smooth, beardless, jolly old dog of an imposter in whom I shall in no wise put faith.   And besides, the Eugenia you speak of has been declared divine and is said to have been placed in the heavens among the constellations.   Her consecrated statue stands in the temple, and you will fare ill indeed if you continue in your sacrilegious declaration.

"The statue you speak of was kissed by a certain man the past night," replied Eugenia in a low voice, casting an inquisitive glance at Aquilinus, who stood astounded and gazed upon her as upon one endowed with superhuman knowledge.   How can the same man be so cruel as to torture the original of the statue?"

Aquilinus fought down his confusion, seemed not to hear the words and continued coldly and severely: "In short, for the honor of the poor monks, who seem innocent, I can and will not believe that you are a woman.   Prepare for death. Your statements have failed to satisfy me."

"Then Heaven help me!" cried Eugenia, and sank to the floor like a white rose broken by the storm.   Aquilinus caught her up in his arms, pressed her to his bosom, while his hot tears fell upon her beautiful head. He kissed her lips I dare say three or four times and left the room, locking the door behind him.

Bearing Eugenia's cowl in his hand, he took himself back to the waiting crowd, whom he addressed thus: "This is indeed a strange affair. You monks are guiltless and may return to your cloister. Your abbot was a demon who had planned to destroy you. Here, take his cowl with you and preserve it as a memento. After the evil spirit had, in my sight, transformed his shape most incredibly, he dissolved into thin air before my very eyes and disappeared. And this woman who sought to destroy you, through the demon, has thereby fallen under suspicion of witchcraft, and shall be cast into prison. Now all of you betake yourselves home and be of good cheer."

All were astonished at this speech, and looked in fear at the garment of the demon. The widow turned pale and covered her face, thereby giving sufficient evidence of her guilt.

The good monks rejoiced at their victory, and wended their way gratefully homeward carrying the cowl, but never dreaming how sweet a kernel had but just been enclosed within it.

The widow was led to prison, and Aquilinus with his most trusted servant travelled the city over, calling at the shops dealing in women's clothing and buying a large amount of the most costly apparel, which was carried by the slave to the consul's house as secretly and quickly as possible.

Noiselessly Aquilinus stepped into the room in which he had left Eugenia. There she lay quite charmingly upon a divan, sleeping soundly, as might be expected of one recuperating from great hardship. As he sat by her side softly stroking her close-cropped hair and laughing to himself at the sight of her monk's tonsure, which was partly hidden by a black velvet cap, she awoke and gazed about her with wondering eyes.

"Will you be my wife?" he pleaded in gentle tones. Whereupon she answered neither yea nor nay, but hid her blushes in the folds of the purple robe in which she lay wrapped.

Then Aquilinus brought the garments and jewels, everything that a gentlewoman of that day might need to clothe herself from head to toe. Thereupon he left the room.

After sunset of the same day he drove with her, accompanied only by a trusted servant, to one of his country villas, which lay charmingly isolated in the shade of a great wood. Here they were quietly wedded, and although love was late in coming, the time did not seem lost to them because of thankful hearts for the great happiness they found in each other's presence.

Aquilinus spent his time in the performance of his civic duties, hastening away, however, at the close of the day to his villa and his young wife, with the fastest of steeds. Only on stormy or rainy days, now and then, was he fond of hastening home unannounced earlier in the afternoon, to cheer his love, who in true housewifely fashion now gave herself up to the study of married life and its pleasures with the same ardor that she had formerly bestowed on the study of philosophy and Christian asceticism.

When her hair had again grown to its natural length, Aquilinus took his wife back to Alexandria, and adducing a fitting explanation and story, restored her to her astonished parents,—whereupon they celebrated a splendid wedding.

Her father was surprised, to be sure, to find in his daughter, instead of an Immortal and a heavenly constellation, a simple, loving housewife, and he witnessed the removal of the consecrated statue with some regret. However, the joy of finding his daughter in the body, more beautiful and lovely than ever, was uppermost.

Aquilinus had the statue placed in the most splendid apartment of his residence, but refrained henceforth from kissing it, since he now had the living original close at hand.

After Eugenia had sufficiently acquainted herself with the ins and outs of wedded life, she turned this knowledge to good account in that she converted her husband to Christianity, and continuing always in the bonds of tenderest love, she rested not until Aquilinus had publicly confessed to her faith.

The legend now goes on to relate how the whole family returned to Rome at the time when the anti-Christian Valerian had come to the throne, and how during the persecutions of the Christians, Eugenia became famed as a standard-bearer and martyr of the faith, and proved the full strength of her mind and heart.

Her influence over Aquilinus was so great that he had even permitted the two Hyacinths to accompany her to Rome, where they, too, were crowned with the crown of martyrdom. Their intercession is said to be beneficial for indolent girl pupils who have fallen behind in their studies.

THE VIRGIN AND THE EVIL ONE

Friend, rise and look about;
Satan attempts each hour,
And should he find thee out,
Then thou art in his power.
—Angelus Silesius.

COUNT GIBIZO possessed a very beautiful wife, a magnificent castle and so many great estates that he was considered one of the richest and happiest lords of the country. That he appreciated this reputation is shown by the Christian benevolence which he exercised to a high degree as well as by his keeping a brilliant circle of friends of whom his good and beautiful wife, Bertrade, was the most shining luminary.

He founded and endowed cloisters and hospices, beautified churches and chapels, and on high festival days fed hundreds of the poor. In truth, he was never content unless dozens of guests were daily and hourly present at the castle to spend their time in feasting, and in singing the praises of their lord and master. Unless thus surrounded, his dwelling, however magnificent it was, seemed to him lonely and forsaken.

But with such prodigal liberality even great wealth must finally be exhausted, and thus it happened that the count was obliged to sell his estates one by one to satisfy his love of great munificence. But the deeper he was plunged into debt the more did he increase his gifts and his feasts to the poor, seeking in this way once more to win the favor of heaven.

At last he was thoroughly impoverished, and his now desolate castle was fast crumbling into ruins. Invalid, meaningless deeds and charters which he still continued to write and bestow upon his friends, as in his days of plenty, brought him only scorn and ridicule. And if peradventure he was able to entice a tattered beggar to his castle, the mendicant cast the dish of poor soup that was offered him disdainfully at his feet and left the domain.

In these troublous times the beauty of his wife, Bertrade, alone, remained unchanged; indeed, the more desolate the house, the more resplendent was she. Yea, she even seemed to grow in grace, loveliness, and goodness of heart, the poorer Gibizo became, until she seemed the embodiment of all the blessings of heaven, and thousands of men envied the count this one remaining treasure.

Gibizo alone took no note of this. The more Bertrade sought to encourage him and to lighten his poverty, the more did he fail to appreciate her. Finally he lapsed into a bitter and stubborn melancholy and withdrew entirely from the society of men.

Now, on a beautiful Easter morning, when in years gone by Gibizo had been accustomed to see throngs of happy people streaming to his castle, the shame of it all fell especially heavy on his heart. He would not even attend divine worship, and knew not how to spend the festive holiday-time.

Smiling through her tears, the wife pleaded with him in vain not to allow himself to be crushed by misfortune, but to accompany her undismayed to church. He thrust her aside almost rudely and hied him away to the woods until the Easter-tide should have passed.

Over hill and dale he wandered until he came to a primeval wilderness where great shaggy firs enclosed a lake, upon the surface of which the mighty tree-trunks were mirrored at full length. The scene was dark and sombre; the earth about the lake was overgrown with fantastic, fringy mosses, so soft and heavy that they did not resound to the tread.

Here Gibizo sat down to mutter against God.

His misfortune weighed heavily upon him. He could no longer even stay his hunger, although he had joyfully fed thousands in his time—for all of which God seemed to have repaid him with the scorn and the ingratitude of the world.

Suddenly he saw in the middle of the lake the tall form of a man in a boat. The lake was small; he could easily survey its entire extent, and he could not understand whence the boatman had so suddenly come. But there he was, and with one stroke of the oar he landed the craft at the feet of the knight. Before the latter was able to utter a word the stranger inquired why he appeared so gloomy.

In spite of the strikingly splendid appearance of the stranger, there was an expression of deep unhappiness about his mouth and eyes that awakened Gibizo's confidence and led him to pour into the willing ear all his misfortunes and his pent-up anger.

"What a fool you are," cried the stranger. "Why, you possess a treasure, greater than all you have lost! If I had your wife, all the riches, the churches, the cloisters, and all the beggars in the world might be hanged!"

"Give me these again, and, for all I care, you

may have my wife," retorted Gibizo with a bitter laugh. Whereupon the stranger replied in a trice: "Good, it's a bargain! Look beneath your wife's pillow; there you will find money enough to last you your entire lifetime; enough to build a cloister every day and to feed a thousand people, should you live even to be a hundred years old. In return, bring your wife to this spot without fail on Walpurgis-night."

At these words there shot out from his dark eyes so fiery a gleam that it extended like two red streaks of light over the count's shoulder and shone on the moss and the trunks of the firs beyond.

And now Gibizo understood with whom he was dealing; yet he accepted the offer.

The stranger again plied his oar and made for the middle of the lake, where man and boat sank out of sight with a din like the clanging of many brazen bells.

Chilled with fear, Gibizo hastened by the shortest route to his castle, where he at once inspected Bertrade's couch, and there, beneath her pillow, he found an old book, which he was unable to read. But as he turned the pages, pieces of gold fell out. No sooner had he discovered this than he hastened away to the deepest dungeon of the castle-tower, and there, all by himself, during the Easter holidays, he leaved out of the interesting book a pile of gold sufficient for all of his present needs.

Once more Gibizo made his appearance among his fellows. He redeemed all of his lost possessions, called in workmen to renovate and remodel his castle on a grander scale than ever, and granted largesses on all hands like a prince who has just come to his regency.

The greatest of his beneficences was the founding of a magnificent abbey, planned to accommodate five hundred of the most pious and celebrated monks, virtually a city of saints and scribes, in the midst of which he intended his own final resting place to be. The latter plan he deemed wise in view of the welfare of his soul, but since he had made other plans for his wife's future, a sepulchre for her was not provided.

At noon of the day before Walpurgis he ordered the horses saddled, and requesting his wife to mount her white palfrey, he pretended that she was to take a long journey with him. At the same time he forbade that any squire or servant attend them.

Now a great fear began to creep over the good woman, and, trembling from head to foot, she spoke false to her husband for the first time, alleging that she was not well and begging him to allow her to remain at home.

Since she had, however, only shortly before, been heard singing to herself, Gibizo became angry at the falsehood, and he made himself believe that now he was doubly justified in what he was planning. He therefore insisted that she attire herself in her most beautiful robe and accompany him on the ride, which she did, without even knowing whither they were bound.

When they had travelled about half the distance, they came to a small chapel which Bertrade had erected and dedicated to the service of the Virgin. She had built it partly out of sympathy for a poor old architect who was of a rather morose and unamiable disposition, and whom consequently no one was inclined to employ, least of all Gibizo, who was fond of having people come to him in a supplicating and reverential manner.

Bertrade had employed him without Gibizo's knowledge, and the unfortunate craftsman had, by way of showing his appreciation, carved a beautiful statue of the Virgin and placed it on the altar.

Bertrade now expressed a desire to enter the chapel for a moment to offer up a prayer. Gibizo acquiesced, for, thought he, it will soon stand her in good stead. She dismounted accordingly, and while her spouse waited without, she entered, and, kneeling down before the altar, commended herself to the protection of her heavenly guardian.

While in this posture, a deep sleep stole over her, and the Virgin, descending from the altar and taking on the form and garb of the sleeper, stepped briskly out from the chapel, mounted the horse, and continued by the side of the count in Bertrade's stead.

And now the wretch attempted to deceive his wife and to lull her into a sense of security by diverting her thoughts with a great show of friendly attention. He spoke to her glibly of many things, the Virgin making soft and low answer, and by her sweet prattle leading him to believe that she was abandoning all fear.

In this way they arrived at the wilderness by the lake, above which the fallow clouds of evening hung. There stood the shaggy firs, their purple buds glowing in the sunset light as only the rarest springtime shows them. In the neighboring thicket the nightingale moaned its weird song, like to the sound of organ and cymbal, while from out the firs rode the stranger, upon a steed black as night, clothed in rich, knightly garb, his long sword hanging by his side.

He approached very gallantly, at the same time, however, shooting so terrible a glance upon Gibizo that his flesh began to creep. But beyond this no one seemed to scent evil, not even the horses, for they remained calm. Gibizo tossed his wife's reins to the stranger and galloped away without even looking back at her. The knight seized the reins with eager hand and away they flew through the firs, the veil and cloak of the fair lady flapping and fluttering in the breeze. Over hill and dale and running streams they sped, the horses' hoofs hardly touching the crests of the waves.

Before them, in the gloaming, driven on in the mad swirl, rolled a rose-scented cloud, while the invisible nightingale flew on before, alighting now and then on a tree, singing her song right lustily on the evening air.

Finally hills and forests came to an end and they galloped out upon a broad heath, in the midst of which, and as if from a great distance, they heard again the song of the bird, although round about them neither shrub nor tree was anywhere to be seen upon which she might have alighted.

Suddenly the knight reined in his steed, sprang

from the saddle, and with the demeanor of a perfect cavalier, helped the lady to dismount.

Barely had her foot touched the earth when up about them there sprang to the height of a man a garden of rose-bushes and a beautiful fountain surrounded by seats, over all of which the starry heaven shone so brightly that you could read by its light. The fountain was in the form of a great, round basin, within which a number of imps were made to represent a white marble group of beautiful, sylph-like forms. Shimmering streams of water, of which no one but their lord and master knew whence it came, poured from their hands. The plash of the water was as music to the ear, for each jet had a sound of its own, and the whole swelled into a sweet harmony like that of an orchestra of stringed instruments. A harmonica of the waters, it seemed, in whose chords vibrated all the sweets of the first night of May. With it mingled and blended the beautiful forms of the nymphs, for the whole was not stationary, but moved and changed panorama-like.

Not ungraciously did the strange cavalier now conduct his lady to the garden-bench and invite her to be seated. Then seizing her hand vehemently, he said in a voice that penetrated to the heart: "I am the eternally Solitary One who fell from high heaven. Only the love of a good woman in the night of May allows me for a time to forget Paradise and gives me strength to bear the eternal damnation. Be mine, and I will make you immortal and give you power to do good and prevent evil, as you may desire."

With that he cast himself passionately upon the breast of the beautiful woman, who smilingly awaited him. But at that moment the Virgin took on her divine form and gripping the now captive traitor she held him in her white arms as in a vise.

Instantly the garden, the fountain and the nightingale disappeared, and the ingenious imps of the living picture took flight like evil spirits amid fearful cries of anguish, leaving their master in the lurch, wrestling with titanic strength to loosen himself from the agonizing embrace, yet not even so much as uttering a sound.

The Virgin struggled, and gripped her adversary fast, although she had to summon all of her strength to do so. Her plan aimed at nothing short of carrying the outwitted devil straight to heaven, there, to his great discomfiture, to bind him to a door-post amid the laughter of the saints.

But now the Evil One changed his tactics. For

a time he remained quiet; then he assumed the beautiful form that he had possessed when he was the foremost of the angels, with the result that it became a comparison of beauty between him and the Virgin.

She set herself off as well as she might, but though she glittered like Venus, the beautiful star of the evening, he shone like Lucifer, the bright star of the morning, and thus the dark heath was made to gleam and sparkle as though the heavens themselves had descended in all of their glory.

When now the Virgin saw that she had undertaken more than she could accomplish, and felt her powers waning, she contented herself with releasing the enemy, upon his promise to renounce his designs upon the Countess Bertrade, whereupon the heavenly and the satanic beauties flew away in different directions with tumultuous noise.

Somewhat fatigued, the Virgin returned to her chapel, while the Evil One, paralyzed in all his limbs and unable to undergo further transformation, dragged himself off over the sand, much the worse for wear, and looking the disordered embodiment of grief. Thus badly did he fare in his proposed love-hour.

Meantime Gibizo, after leaving his sweet wife,

had ridden astray in the falling dusk, and horse and rider had fallen into a deep abyss, where he was dashed upon the rocks with such violence that he straightway yielded up his wicked spirit.

Bertrade, in the chapel, continued in slumber until the morning sun of the first day of May began to climb the eastern hills, when she awoke, much astonished at the length of her nap.

She prayed the Ave, stepped out from the chapel, and there stood her horse just as she had left it.

She did not stop to await her husband's return, but rode quickly and cheerfully homeward, for she divined that she had escaped some great danger.

Soon the remains of the late count were brought to the castle. Bertrade had him buried with all honors, and besides she paid for many masses to be read for his soul's repose, but all of her love for him had been crushed from her heart, although toward all others she remained as kind and loving as ever.

In the course of time, Bertrade's heavenly protectress gave her another husband, one more worthy than Gibizo of so devoted a wife, and these events took place as will be related in the following legend.

THE VIRGIN IN THE RÔLE OF KNIGHT

The tent of God, Mary is called, and God's throne;
An ark, burg, tower, house, a spring, a sea, garden, mirror,
A tree, a star, the moon, the morning-red, a mountain.
Can she be all of these? She calls a world her own.

—Angelus Silesius.

GIBIZO had in addition to his former possessions acquired many more, and thus Bertrade held sway over a great earldom, and became famed throughout the German empire for her riches as well as for her great beauty.

Since she was modesty itself, and was very friendly towards all men, this treasure of a woman was thought easy to be won by all the enterprising and the timid, the bold and the bashful, the great and the small noblemen of the realm, and every man who saw her wondered why in all the world he had not already made her his wife. But more than one year had gone by and still there was no man to whom she had really given reason to hope.

The Emperor himself heard of her, and desiring that so important a fief as hers should come into the hands of a good man, he decided to pay a visit to the far-famed Bertrade, informed her of his intention by letter, and sent the message by a young knight, Zendelwald by name, who happened to be bound that way. Zendelwald was received graciously by Bertrade, and entertained like all others who chanced to be her guests at her castle. He was charmed, and gazed upon the beautiful halls, the battlements and the gardens in great respect, and incidentally he fell in love with the fair possessor.

But, strange as it may seem, he did not tarry an hour longer than his mission required. As soon as he had concluded his errand he bade the countess a brief farewell and rode away, the only one of all who had ever visited Bertrade, to acknowledge himself unable to win this fair prize.

Zendelwald was slow of speech and action. When his mind and heart had once taken possession of a project, a thing which he always did with the zest and enthusiasm native to him, he could not find it within himself to take the first step towards carrying it out, since the matter seemed to him accomplished, once he had settled it in his own mind.

And so, although he was very fond of talking about things when there was nothing immediately to be realized, he never spoke the word which might have sealed his fortune at the right moment.

Moreover, his thoughts not only outran his speech, but his hand as well, with the result that he had been nearly conquered several times in armed combat because he had neglected to deal the decisive blow at the proper moment, in his mind's eye already seeing his opponent at his feet. Thus his manner of fighting excited great curiosity at the tournaments, since at the outset he hardly moved or exerted himself at all, and only when hard pressed did he put forth a great and final effort, thereby generally winning the conflict.

Deep in thought, the object of which was beautiful Bertrade, Zendelwald now rode home to his castle, which lay in a solitary mountain forest. Charcoal-burners and wood-cutters were his only subjects, and thus his lonely mother awaited his return as usual with great impatience, wondering whether he might this time bring his good fortune home with him in the shape of a lovely wife.

But if Zendelwald was a dreamer, his mother was not. She was active and resolute, without, however, deriving much advantage from these characteristics, since she had always displayed them so unpleasantly to others that they no longer proved themselves effective.

When a girl, she had sought to capture a husband as soon as might be, and therefore had pursued her matrimonial chances so hotly that in her haste she hit upon the worst possible choice in the person of a rash and foolhardy fellow who squandered his inheritance and came to a premature grave, leaving her a young widow in poverty, and burdened with a son who was slow to make his fortune.

The sole sustenance of the small household consisted of wild fruit and game and the milk of a couple of goats. Zendelwald's mother was a great huntress. With her crossbow she brought down wild doves and woodcocks to her heart's content. She caught trout, too, in the neighboring streams, and with her own hands made the necessary repairs in the castle walls with stone and mortar.

Even now she was returning from the chase, and as she hung a hare in the window of her kitchen, she glanced down across the valley and caught sight of her son riding up the path. Overjoyed at the sight, she hastened to lower the drawbridge, for Zendelwald had not been home for months.

She began at once to quiz him whether perchance he had lit upon and brought with him some little pinion or tail-feather of the Bird of Fortune on which it might be wise to keep a hold. But when he related the usual unimportant happenings of his warlike expedition she shook her head angrily, and when he finally mentioned his mission to the charming and beautiful Bertrade and was loud in his praise of her grace and beauty, she called him a laggard and a lazy-bones because of his ignominious departure from the countess' domains.

Moreover, when she perceived, as she soon did, that Zendelwald thought of nothing but his distant, noble lady, she became doubly incensed to learn that in spite of his deep regard for Bertrade, he had been at a loss to know what to do or to say and that his love was a hindrance to him rather than an impulse towards action.

From this moment Zendelwald's pathway was a thorny one. His mother sulked and stormed. To quiet her anger, and by way of diversion, she set to work with her own hands to repair the crumbling roof of the castle tower until our good Zendelwald became alternately hot and cold with fear at seeing her clambering about on the high roofs. She was in a fine fury and continued to throw pieces of broken tile to the earth so furiously that she almost killed a strange horseman who chanced to be entering the castle gate to petition for a night's lodging.

However, this man succeeded in appeasing the austere dame with his tales of adventure, told over the evening meal. Especially did he catch her fancy when he dwelt on the Emperor's visit at the castle of the beautiful Bertrade and on the festivals which followed fast one upon another's heels. "The charming woman," related he, "is being incessantly urged by the King and his grandees to select a husband from among the noblemen of the realm. But she has had recourse to the subterfuge of convoking a great tournament, and has promised to bestow her hand upon the victor, for she believes firmly that her protectress, the Holy Virgin, will intervene, and guide the arm of the chosen one."

"Now, this is an adventure for you," the stranger concluded, turning to Zendelwald; "A handsome young man of your stamp ought to aspire to the very best to be had in the world. Rumor has it, too, that the lady is possessed of a firm belief that in this way some unsurmised good fortune will come to her, some impecunious but doughty knight on whom she may bestow all of her love, for she is much averse to the great counts and vain suitors known to her."

When the stranger had departed, Zendelwald's mother said: "Now I'll wager that no one but Bertrade herself has sent this messenger to entice you on to the right trail, my dear Zendelwald. That's as plain as can be. How otherwise should this queer bird who has just drunk our last jug of wine have come to this forest?"

At this Zendelwald struck up a great laugh, and louder and louder he laughed, partly, no doubt, because of her maternal fancies, partly because it pleased him. The mere thought that Bertrade might desire him as her husband shook him with laughter.

But the mother, believing he was laughing her to scorn, went into a great rage and cried: "Now hear me. My curse upon you, if you do not obey me and betake yourself on the way at once to win this woman. Do not return without her, or I will never look upon you again. And if you come without her, I'll take my cross-bow and leave this spot, to find a resting-place beneath the sod, where I may be unmolested by your stupidity."

Now there was no alternative for Zendelwald. For the sake of the family peace he laid on his armor, took his weapons, and commending himself to the protection of Heaven, rode away in the direction of Bertrade's castle, without, however, seriously purposing ever to arrive there.

He held pretty closely to the course, nevertheless, and the nearer he drew to the place, the more clearly did the thought shape itself that he as well as any one might undertake the thing, and that after he should have overcome his rivals it would not be risking his life to venture a dance with the fair lady of his heart.

In his imagination, the adventure unrolled itself step by step and he fairly revelled in it. Indeed, for days, while riding through the verdant fields of summer, he held sweet concourse with his beloved, communicating to her the most charming fancies, which made her face radiant with womanly joy. But all of this was in his mind.

Even now, as he was again depicting some joyful event in his imagination, he saw along the blue mountain-ridge the towers and battlements and the gilded parapets of her castle sparkle and gleam in the morning sun, and he was so frightened by the sight that all his dream-fabric vanished, leaving him as timid and irresolute as before.

Involuntarily he reined in his steed and looked

about him, after the fashion of the irresolute, for a manner of escape. As he did so he caught sight of a small chapel, the same which Bertrade had erected to the honor of the Virgin and in which she had had her long sleep. He decided to stop there to collect and strengthen himself a bit before the altar. More especially did he feel the need of this since it was the very day on which the tournament was to be held.

As he entered, a priest was saying mass. There were only two or three people in attendance, and the presence of the knight shed not a little lustre on the small congregation. But when the service was over and priest and sacristan had left the church, Zendelwald felt so comfortable in his little nook that he soon fell asleep, quite forgetting both tournament and lady love, unless perchance he saw them in his dreams.

And again the Virgin descended from the altar, and taking on Zendelwald's form and armor, she mounted his horse and rode away in his stead, with closed visor—a Brunhild in bearing—towards the castle.

After riding some distance, she came upon a pile of old rubbish and dry branches which attracted her attention. Peering closer, she noticed the tail of a reptile protruding from under the mass. It was the Evil One, who, still filled with his base passion, had continued to slink about the neighborhood of the castle and who at the approach of the Virgin had taken refuge under the rubbish heap. Apparently without noticing him she rode by, but by a clever maneuver made her horse's hind hoof strike the projecting tail. With a hiss, the Evil One started up and away and was not seen again in the neighborhood.

Amused by this little escapade, she rode merrily on towards the castle. When she arrived there, the tournament was almost over. Only two of the most powerful knights still remained and were about to decide the outcome of the tournament between them.

Slowly and in a careless manner, after the fashion of Zendelwald, the Virgin rode into the lists, and for a moment she seemed undecided whether she should enter the conflict or not.

"Oh, here comes Zendelwald, late as usual," the people called, and the two knights who remained on the field said: "What will he here? Let us put him out of the way, before settling the matter."

The one was called Sir Guhl, the Speedy, because he was fond of wheeling his horse about like a whirlwind, and of confusing and conquering his opponent by a hundred sly turns and tricks.

With him the supposed Zendelwald had first to try consequences. Sir Guhl had a pitchy black moustache, the ends of which were twisted smartly and stood perpendicularly upright, so stiffly that they were able to support two small silver bells that were fastened to them and which rang whenever he moved his head. He called these bells the chimes of his enemies' dismay, and the chimes of his lady-love's delight. His shield shone in changing colors, accordingly as he turned it this way or that, and so adept was he in bringing about this play of color that the eyes of the onlookers were dazzled by it. And finally, his helmet plumes consisted of a great rooster's tail.

The second opponent was called Sir Maus, the Innumerable, which epithet he intended to mean that he was to be regarded as a great and numberless army. As evidence of his great strength he had let the hair grow from his nostrils to the length of six inches, and had it braided in two small braids which hung down over his mouth and were adorned with dainty bows of red ribbon. Over his armor he wore a large loose-fitting cloak which was made of thousands of mole-skins, and which almost covered both horse and rider. A great outstretched bat's wing served him as a crest, from below which he shot out menacing glances through the narrow slits of his eyes.

The signal for the contest with Sir Guhl was given. He rode up to and about the Virgin, encircling her with increasing rapidity in order to blind her with his shield, all the while essaying numerous blows with his lance.

But the Virgin continued in the centre of the field as if rooted to the spot, and seemed only to ward off his attack with shield and lance, wheeling her horse with great skill as she did so, and managing continually to face the enemy.

Guhl, noticing this, suddenly rode off some distance; then turning, he rushed upon his antagonist with lance atilt to strike her to the ground.

The Virgin awaited him, motionless, and rider and steed seemed modelled in steel, so immovably did they stand. Poor Guhl, who knew not that he was closing in with a higher power, lit upon her lance and was thrown from his saddle to the earth in a trice, while his own weapon was shattered upon her shield like a reed.

Immediately she sprang from her horse and, placing her knee upon his breast, pinned him to the ground. With a stroke of her dagger she cut off the moustaches with their bells, and fastened them to her sword-belt, just as the flourish of trumpets greeted her, or rather Zendelwald, as the victor.

Now it was Sir Maus's turn. With great verve he galloped into the field, his cloak flying in the air like a menacing cloud of gray.

But Virgin-Zendelwald, who only now seemed to be warming up to the contest, dashed towards him with an equal show of strength, unseating him easily with her first blow. And when he sprang up and drew his sword, she also sprang from her horse, ready to continue the struggle on foot.

He was soon dazed by the rapid sword-blows that she dealt him on head and shoulders, while he, holding out his cloak with his left hand to screen himself, sought if possible to cast it over the head of his opponent.

But the Virgin caught a corner of the cloak upon the point of her sword, and with a swift turn of her hand wrapped Sir Maus, the Innumerable, up in it from head to foot with such graceful dexterity that he lay struggling upon the earth like a great wasp that has been enmeshed by a spider.

Thereupon she gave him so thorough a drubbing with the flat of her sword that his mantle was resolved into its component parts, and the thousands of mole-skins, flying this way and that, amid the general laughter of the spectators, almost shut out the light of the sun. After a time the knight emerged from the hubbub and hobbled away, a crushed man; not, however, before his conqueror had deprived him of his ribboned moustachios.

And thus the Virgin, in the person of Zendelwald, stood upon the field of combat, the sole victor.

She now raised her visored helmet, strode up to the queen of the tournament, and, bending her knee before her, laid the trophies of victory at her feet.

This done, she arose, and looking a bolder Zendelwald than that gentleman ever had the boldness to look, without, however, sacrificing any of his modesty, she greeted Bertrade with a look the effect of which upon a woman's heart she well knew. In short, she deported herself in such manner in her rôle of lover as well as knight, that Bertrade did not retract her promise, made before the tournament, but yielded to the advice of the Emperor, who was happy to see so valiant and noble a man come into the earldom.

They now took their way in great procession to the grove of high towering lindens, where a banquet had been prepared. Bertrade sat between the

Emperor and her chosen Zendelwald, and it was fortunate that the Emperor had, at his side, another pretty companion, for Zendelwald did not allow his bride much time to speak to others, so cleverly and tenderly did he entertain her. Evidently he was whispering sweet nothings into her ear, since every now and then deep blushes overspread her radiant face and neck.

Joy reigned supreme. In the heavy-foliaged arches overhead, the birds vied with the music of the festive board. A butterfly alighted on the Emperor's golden crown, while the goblets of wine, as if by a special blessing of heaven, gave forth a fragrance as of violets and mignonette.

Bertrade was very happy, and while Zendelwald held her hand in his, her thoughts ascended to her divine Protectress, and she offered up a fervent prayer of thanksgiving in her heart.

The Virgin, who, as we know, was sitting at her side in the person of Zendelwald, read the prayer in her heart and was so gratified with the piety of her fledgling that she embraced her passionately and impressed a kiss upon her lips, filling the lovely woman with heavenly rapture, for when the celestials take to making sweets they make them very sweet.

The Emperor, however, and the rest of the company, applauded the supposed Zendelwald, and raising their beakers drank to the health of the beautiful couple.

Meantime, the real Zendelwald awoke from his inopportune sleep, and saw the sun already so high that he thought the tournament must be over.

Although he was now fortunately delivered from the affair, he felt unhappy and sad, for really he had desired very much to win the lady's love, and besides, he now no longer dared return to his mother, and thus he decided to set out upon never-ending wanderings until death should release him from his useless existence. Only once more he wished to look upon the loved woman that he might fix her image upon his heart forever to remind him of his loss.

He wended his way towards the castle accordingly, and as he drew near he heard all lips proclaiming the praise and the good fortune of a certain poor knight Zendelwald, who was said to have gained the prize. Painfully curious to learn who this Zendelwald might be, he dismounted and made his way through the crowd to an elevated spot near the edge of the garden, from where he was able to survey the entire festive scene.

He saw the face of Bertrade beaming in jewelled splendor near the sparkling crown of the Emperor, and next to her, to his utter amazement, he saw the exact likeness of his own person.

He gazed upon the scene as one transfixed, until he saw his double embrace and kiss the beautiful bride; then, unmindful of the general joy, he strode with a steady tread through the crowd and stood close behind the couple, consumed with a strange feeling of jealousy.

At the same moment his counterpart disappeared from Bertrade's side and she, looking about for him and catching sight of Zendelwald behind her, cooed a joyful little laugh of love and said: "Are you there, my love? Come, remain close by me," and she seized his hand and drew him to her side.

Zendelwald sat down, accordingly, and, to test what seemed to him to be a dream, he seized a goblet of wine standing before him and emptied it at one draught. The wine was good; it poured life and confidence into his veins, and as his spirits rose, he turned and gazed into the eyes of the radiant woman, who now took up the conversation where it had been interrupted.

But when Bertrade spoke words that he seemed

to have heard before, and to which he made answer in words which he too seemed to have spoken somewhere previously, Zendelwald hardly knew what to make of it all. And, indeed, after a time he noticed that his predecessor must have said the very things which he himself had imagined himself saying to her on his journey hither, and which he now deliberately continued in order to see what the outcome of the whole affair might be.

But there were no untoward results; in fact, their conversation became more and more pleasant, and when the sun had set, torches were lighted and the entire company betook themselves to the great hall of the castle to give themselves up to the pleasures of the dance.

The first dance with the bride was the Emperor's privilege. Thereupon Zendelwald claimed her, but they had taken only three or four turns about the hall, when his rosy partner seized him by the hand and led him to a quiet turret chamber which lay flooded with the light of the moon. Now, seated by his side, she embraced him tenderly, caressing his tawny beard and thanking him for his coming and for his love.

But honest Zendelwald now wanted to know whether he was dreaming or waking; so he questioned her as to the real state of affairs, especially concerning his double.

For a long time she failed to understand what he was driving at, until finally it began to dawn upon her. Zendelwald related what had befallen him and told of his experiences from the time he had entered the chapel; how he had fallen asleep, thereby arriving too late for the tournament.

Now Bertrade understood, and she recognized the hand of her protectress for the second time in her life. Even more than heretofore she now regarded her brave knight as a gift of Heaven, and so thankful was she that she pressed the sturdy gift doughtily to her heart and returned the sweet kiss that she had received from Heaven itself.

From this time on Zendelwald laid off all his indolent ways and his dreamy manner and became quick of speech and action, not only towards the loved woman but towards all the world. And he became renowned in the empire, and the Emperor was as much pleased with him as was his wife.

Zendelwald's mother honored the young couple with her presence at the wedding, and she came high ahorse and as proudly as though Fortune had smiled upon her all the days of her life. She continued to administer the affairs of her own estates, and remained, until a ripe old age, in her great forests, devoted to the chase.

Once a year Bertrade insisted upon being accompanied by Zendelwald to his little, obscure, paternal castle, there to coo with her lover as tenderly as the wild doves on the great trees about the old haunt. And never once did they neglect to enter the chapel and to offer up their prayers to the Virgin, who continued in her place on the altar, as quiet and serene as though she had never been known to forsake it.

DOROTHEA'S FLOWER-BASKET

But to lose oneself thus means to find oneself.
—Franciscus Ludovicus Blosius.

O N THE southern shore of the Pontus
Euxinus, not far from the mouth of the
river Halys, there lay, in the light of the
brightest of spring mornings, a Roman villa. A
breeze from the northeast wafted grateful coolness
over the gardens from the waters of the sea, re-
freshing heathens and Christians alike, and caus-
ing all to feel as blithe as the foliage that trembled
in the spring breeze.

In a shady bower by the shore of the sea, stood
two young people, a handsome youth and the fairest
of maidens. She held in her hand a beautiful, large
cut-glass vase of translucent red and seemed to be
inviting the young man to admire it. As she did
so, the light of the morning sun, reflected by the
vase upon her face, vied with the blushes on her
cheek.

Dorothea was the maiden's name. She was the
daughter of a patrician, and it was well known that
her hand was being sought in marriage by Fabricius, the governor of the province of Cappadocia.
But since he was a bitter persecutor of the Chris-

tians, and Dorothea's parents were kindly disposed towards the new faith, they resisted, as far as they dared, the suit of the powerful inquisitor.

Now one must not suppose that Dorothea's parents wished to embroil their children in controversies concerning the faith, nor to barter away their hearts as the purchase price of new proselytes to the Christian religion; they were too noble and liberal-minded to do that. They simply felt that a religious inquisitor would certainly turn out but a poor lover and husband.

Dorothea did not trouble herself about these aspects at all. She felt herself quite secure against the blandishments of the governor. The fact was, she loved his private secretary, Theophilus, who even at this moment stood at her side, casting perplexed but admiring glances at the ruby vase.

Theophilus was a well-bred and handsome young man of Greek descent who had risen, in spite of adverse circumstances, and who enjoyed the respect of all who knew him. But his years of poverty had imprinted upon his character a trait of mistrust and of taciturnity, and since he had made his way in the world entirely by his own efforts, he was rarely able to make himself believe that anyone had his interests especially at heart.

He was passionately devoted to Dorothea, but the fact that the first man in Cappadocia was paying suit to her deterred him from entertaining any hope for himself, and not for any consideration would he have consented to become the laughing-stock in a race with that great gentleman.

Nevertheless, Dorothea sought to accomplish her ends and for the present to enjoy the pleasure of his company as often as possible. And since he seemed always quiet and indifferent, her ardor rose until she even began to make use of doubtful little artifices, as when she tried to arouse his jealousy by seeming to look with favor upon the suit of the governor.

But poor Theophilus had no comprehension of such strategy, and if he had understood, his pride would not have allowed him to show his jealousy.

In spite of himself he was, however, gradually carried away, made uneasy and brought at times to betray his real feelings, but straightway collecting himself, he resumed his usual manner, thus leaving his fair admirer no alternative but to proceed more aggressively and perchance suddenly to enmesh him.

At present he had come to the Black Sea region on business, and Dorothea, as soon as she learned of it, had followed her parents thither to their country villa. Thus she had, by clever planning, succeeded on this morning in inveigling him into the arbor. She intended to have this meeting appear partly as an accident, partly as an evidence of friendship. She hoped, too, that this piece of good fortune, backed by the ingratiating manner which she intended to assume, might induce a cheerful and confiding mood in him.

Thus she happened to be exhibiting to him the vase that her uncle had sent her as a present from Trapezunt, on the anniversary of her patron saint's day. Her face was aglow with joy at having her lover so near her and all to herself, and at being able to delight him with so beautiful a thing as the vase. He too seemed happy. The sun of love was beaming in his heart, smiling on his lips and shining from his eyes.

But along with blooming Eros, the ancients neglected to mention the god of Envy who, at the decisive moment, when Fortune smiles, casts a veil over lovers' eyes and hushes the words of love and troth already on their lips.

When Dorothea placed the vase trustingly in his hands and he asked who had given it to her, a burst of wanton roguishness led her to answer:

"Fabricius," and she felt sure he would not fail to understand the pleasantry.

But since she had not succeeded in intermingling with her smile the requisite touch of sarcasm for the absent Fabricius, which would have made the pleasantry more evident, Theophilus firmly believed that her joyful mood was induced by the recollection of the giver and that he, Theophilus, had made a great mistake by attempting the conquest of a heart that was already won, and was a stranger to him.

Mute with a sense of shame, he cast down his eyes and the trembling of his hands caused the vase to fall to the ground where it was dashed to pieces.

The first shock of this untoward turn caused Dorothea to forget not only her intended pleasantry, but, for the moment, Theophilus as well, and as she bent down to pick up the fragments she exclaimed: "How stupid!" And since she was quite intent upon what she was doing, she failed to notice the change that had come over his face, and not once surmised his misinterpretation of her remark concerning Fabricius.

When she again rose, and quickly collecting herself, turned to address him, Theophilus had already drawn himself up proudly to his full height.

Darkling and seemingly unconcerned, he looked into her eyes; almost scornfully he begged her pardon, and promising a full restitution for the broken vase, bowed and left the garden.

Dorothea turned pale, and with tears gathering in her beautiful eyes followed the tall form of Theophilus as he drew his white toga about him, and inclined his head with its curling locks, as if lost in deep philosophical reflections.

Only the waves of the silvery sea lapped softly in slow beats at the marble steps of the shore. All else was quiet, and Dorothea's small strategies were at an end.

Weeping bitterly, she wended her way slowly to her room, there to hide the fragments of the broken vessel.

Months passed, and the lovers had not met. Theophilus had betaken himself at once to the capital, and when, by autumn, Dorothea also returned, he carefully avoided seeing her. Even the thought of a meeting with her troubled and excited him, and thus their fond young dream seemed forever past and ended.

Now it came about, and quite naturally too, that Dorothea sought solace in the faith of her parents, and they, noticing it, did not neglect to encourage her and to seek to introduce her to the tenets of the new religion.

Meantime the apparently favorable attitude of Dorothea towards the governor had produced its unfortunate effect in that it led Fabricius to renew his suit with increased fervor, as he fully believed he was justified in doing.

But what was his astonishment when Dorothea would not even deign to look upon him, and his presence seemed more distasteful to her than communion with her own sad thoughts. Yet Fabricus was undismayed. In sooth, he increased his attentions, but strangely enough, he began at the same time to assail her new faith, and to mingle his flatteries with thinly veiled threats.

Dorothea, however, confessed her belief openly and fearlessly; and flatly discountenancing his suit, paid no more attention to him.

Theophilus heard of all this and learned too that she was quite unhappy. Most of all did the news that she positively refused to have anything to do with the governor astonish him. Now, although in matters of religion Theophilus was worldly-minded and quite indifferent, he was not at all inimical to the girl's new faith, and actuated by his old-time regard for her, he began gradually to make approaches, in order, if possible, to see or hear how she was faring.

But Dorothea was able in those days to think or do nothing except to speak in the tenderest phrases of a heavenly bridegroom, who was awaiting her in undying glory to present her with the rose of eternal life.

Of course Theophilus did not understand this language. It angered and hurt him and filled his heart with a peculiar, painful jealousy of the unknown god who had infatuated the mind of the poor child, for he was unable to explain the language of the agitated and forsaken woman in any other than the current mythological fashion. But to be jealous of a celestial did not hurt his pride; and his sympathy for a maiden who boasted of relations with the gods, waned.

Still it was only her unrequited love for him that was responsible for this behavior, just as Theophilus himself never ceased to feel the promptings of the old ardor in his heart.

Things went on in this way for a time until Fabricius forcibly intervened. Alleging that he had new imperial orders to prosecute the Christians, he had Dorothea and her parents arrested, but separately incarcerated and examined under torture.

Eager to learn the result, Fabricius came in person and with his own ears heard Dorothea revile the ancient gods and confess Christ as the one and only Lord of the world, whose promised bride she professed to be.

Now the governor was likewise seized with great jealousy. He resolved to destroy her and commanded that she be tortured and, should she continue perverse, executed. Thereupon he departed.

Accordingly she was placed upon an iron grate under which coals were ignited in such fashion that the heat arose but slowly. But Dorothea's delicate body soon began to suffer great agony. She uttered suppressed sobs; her limbs, which were fastened to the iron bars, moved convulsively and tears started from her eyes.

Meanwhile Theophilus, who usually refrained from going near such scenes, had heard of Dorothea's straits and had hastened thither in agitation and solicitude. All unmindful of his own safety, he forced his way through the gaping crowd, and when Dorothea's subdued sobs struck his ear, he snatched a sword from one of the soldiers and with a bound, stood before the bed of torture.

"Thou art in great pain," said he, smiling

through his grief, as he stood about to cut her bonds asunder.

As if suddenly freed from all suffering and filled with the greatest joy, she answered: "And why dost thou think it painful, Theophilus? These are the roses of my beloved bridegroom on which I am reclining, and today is my bridal day."

About her lips there hovered an expression of sweet playfulness and her eyes beamed upon him with an almost heavenly radiance, while a halo of light seemed to transfigure both the girl and her gruesome couch. A solemn stillness ensued; Theophilus' arm faltered; then he cast the sword aside and withdrew, abashed and perplexed, as he had that eventful morning in the garden by the sea.

And now the flame leapt up anew. Dorothea groaned loudly and begged for death. This boon was soon granted her and she was led forth to the place of execution to be beheaded.

With a light step she made her way thither, followed by the thoughtless, clamoring mob. As she was led along, she caught sight of Theophilus, who, standing by the way, never took his eyes from her for a moment. Their glances met. Dorothea paused a moment, and in her sweet voice said: "O Theophilus, if only you knew how beautiful are the rose-gardens of my Lord, into which I shall enter within a few moments, and how fragrant the sweet apples that grow there, you would come with me."

And Theophilus, laughing bitterly, answered "Ah, Dorothea, send me of your roses and apples when you enter into your paradise, will you not?" And she nodded sweetly and continued on her way. Theophilus followed her with his eyes until the cloud of dust, gold-tinted by the rays of the evening sun, which accompanied the procession, faded away in the distance, and the street became again quiet and forsaken.

Then, concealing his face in his toga, to hide his grief, he walked slowly homeward. With wavering step he mounted to the roof of his dwelling, from whence there was an outlook towards the mount Argæus, at the base of which the place of execution lay. Far in the distance he could distinguish clearly the dark, surging mass of human forms, and he extended his arms passionately towards the spot. And now he saw in the light of the setting sun the flash of a descending blade, and he fell headlong as he stood, with his face upon the ground, for at that very moment Dorothea had perished beneath the executioner's sword.

He had not long lain motionless, however, when

a bright shaft of light illumined the falling dusk, the dazzling splendor of it penetrating his closed eyelids like liquid gold, while at the same time the air was filled with sweet fragrance.

As if animated by a new sense of life, the young man arose. Before him stood a wondrously beautiful boy with curly golden locks and dimpled bare feet. He was clothed in a starry garment and held in his luminous hands a small basket, filled with exquisite roses, the like of which he had never seen before, and among the roses there lay three apples of Paradise.

With a naïve and childlike laugh, and yet not without a certain sweet archness, the child said: "Dorothea sends you this," and placing the basket in Theophilus' hands he added, "You are sure you have a firm hold upon it?" then disappeared.

There was no mistake. Theophilus really held the basket in his hand. Upon examination he found in each of the three apples the marks of two dainty teeth, a token which lovers of antiquity were fond of employing. Straightway he placed an apple between his lips, and under the starry heavens, partook with a sweet sadness of the heavenly food.

As he did so, a great longing came over him, and

pressing the basket to his breast and covering it with his cloak, he hastened down from the roof, through the streets and into the palace of the governor, whom he found sitting at meat, seeking to drown his great rage in the undiluted wine of Colchis.

With glowing eyes Theophilus approached him, not, however, disclosing his basket, and in the presence of the entire household addressed him thus: "I confess to the faith of Dorothea whom you have just put to death. It is the only true faith."

"Then you shall follow the witch," cried the governor, springing from his chair, shaken by sudden anger and fierce envy. And the private secretary was beheaded that very hour.

Thus Theophilus was united with Dorothea at once and forever.

She greeted him with the calm look and demeanor of the angels, and like two doves, who, separated for a season by the storm, have been reunited and now wing their way about the nest in great circles, so the reunited lovers glided hand in hand swiftly and without stopping to rest, along the outermost confines of heaven, freed from all the dross of the earthly, and yet perfectly themselves.

Joyously they separated now and strayed far and wide in the infinite realms, each knowing, however, where the other was, and what he thought, and that each enfolded the other and all creation and all being in his love. Again they sought each other, as a longing that knew no sorrow and no impatience possessed them; and when they met they wandered hand in hand or rested in contemplation of each other and of the vast extent of the infinite world.

THE DANCE LEGEND

*O virgin of Israel; thou shalt again be adorned
with thy tabrets, and shalt again go forth in the
dances of them that make merry.*

*Then shall the virgin rejoice in the dance, both
young men and old together.—Jeremiah XXXI, 4,13.*

ACCORDING to Saint Gregory, Musa was
the dancer among the saints. She was a
beautiful girl, of good parentage, and
she served the Virgin zealously. She was possessed
of but one reprehensible trait,—an almost irresist-
ible love of the dance. So ardent was her fondness
for this pastime that when the child was not at her
prayers, she might surely be found dancing. And
in sooth there was no form of dancing she did not
like. She danced with her playmates, with the
children, with the young men, and by herself. She
danced in her chamber, she danced in the halls, she
danced in the gardens and she danced out on the
meadows. And even when she approached the
altar, her carriage was rather the graceful, rythmic
movement of the dance than the prosaic walk, and
she never failed to enjoy a few measures on the
smooth marble slabs before the church door.

Indeed, one day when she was alone in the sanctuary she could not refrain from executing a few figures before the altar, and, as it were, dancing a pretty prayer before the Virgin. So enrapt was she in this that, when a noble looking man danced out towards her, supplementing her figures so skillfully that together they carried out a most beautiful minuet, she imagined herself only dreaming.

The man wore a gown of royal purple and a crown of gold, and his lustrous, wavy, dark beard had the merest suggestion of the silvery hoar of years, like the distant glimmer of starlight.

Above them from the choir-loft resounded sweet music, for there on the parapet sat, or stood, a company of small cherubs playing various instruments, their dimpled little legs hanging down over the coping.

They were gladsome little fellows, and practical too, for they made the stone angels that served as decorative figures on the balcony railing hold their music for them, all except the smallest of them, a chubby-cheeked flute-player, who sat with legs crossed, holding the sheet of music between his pink toes. This little fellow was also most intent upon his work. The rest sat dangling their feet and teasing each other, and now and again one of them would stretch his rustling wings so that you might see the play of colors on them as on the neck of a dove.

But Musa was too engrossed to wonder at all this, until the dance was over, and that was a considerable time, for her jovial partner seemed to take just as much pleasure in it as did Musa, who felt as if transported to the heavens.

But when the music ceased and Musa stood with heaving bosom, fear began to steal over her as she looked in amazement at the man, who seemed neither to breathe more heavily nor to have become in the slightest heated by the dance.

Introducing himself as David, the royal ancestor and at the same time the messenger of the Virgin, he said: "And now, my pretty maid, what say you to spending eternity in one never-ending joyous dance, compared to which the one we have just danced may be called a sorry form of creeping?"

She answered that nothing could give her greater delight, whereupon David replied: "In that case you have only to renounce the dance and all worldly pleasures during your lifetime and to consecrate yourself to penance and spiritual exercises without once wavering or wearying in them."

Taken aback somewhat by this, she asked him whether she must renounce these pleasures entirely.

She even expressed a doubt that there was any dancing in heaven, for, said she, "Everything has its time and place, and the earth seems good enough for dancing, so that heaven must have other uses, otherwise death were entirely superfluous."

But David made clear to her that she was much mistaken, and he proved by many passages of Scripture, as well as by his own example, that dancing was a sacred form of amusement among the blessed. "Now, we want a few more dancers in heaven," said he, "so let us have a quick decision whether or not you will, through temporal renunciation, enter the joys of the blest."

Musa stood irresolute and in doubt, nervously pursing her lips against the tips of her rosy fingers. It did seem hard to give up her favorite pastime and all for the promises of an insecure reward.

But as she stood revolving the matter, suddenly, upon a signal from David, the first measures of an ineffably sweet dance floated out on the stillness of the chapel. The girl stood trembling with joyful agitation, her limbs all a-quiver, but unable to enter into the movement of the dance, for, as she soon perceived, her earthly body was far too cumbrous for such melody. Filled with longing, she placed her hand in that of the king and promised.

In a trice she was alone. The ministering angels had fluttered and rustled away, jostling each other as they flew out through an open window of the chapel, after having in true childlike mischievousness slapped the cheeks of the patient stone cherubs with their rolled-up music sheets, each slap awakening loud echoes in the old church.

Musa walked home with devout step, the heavenly melody still vibrating within her soul. Laying off her pretty clothes, she donned a coarse penitent's garb. Where the trees cast a dense shade, in the rear of her father's garden, a hermit's cell was erected, and within it a moss-covered pallet. Here she lived from that time on, apart from the world,—a penitent and a recluse.

She spent her time in prayer and frequent castigations. Her most severe penance consisted in holding her limbs perfectly quiet, for as soon as a note was sounded without—the song of a bird or the rustling of the leaves—her feet began to twitch for the dance. And since, before she was aware of it, this impulse at times prompted her into a little bound, she had her feet fastened together with a light chain.

Her relatives and friends marvelled day and night at her transformation, but were none the less proud to possess so great a saint, and guarded the hermitage among the trees as the apple of their eye. Many came for advice and for prayers. Especially did they bring young girls who were awkward of bearing, since all whom she touched began forthwith to walk easily and gracefully.

In this way Musa lived in her cell for three years. Towards the end of the third year she had become as light and ethereal as a summer cloud. She lay day and night on her moss-covered bed, her eyes turned wistfully to heaven, where already she believed she could see, through the blue, the golden slippers of the saints dancing down the corridors of heaven.

At last, on a blustering autumn day the news went out that the saint lay dying. She had laid off her dark penitential garb, had clothed herself in a dazzling white bridal gown and lay with folded hands, serenely awaiting the hour of departure.

The garden was filled with throngs of the faithful, the autumn winds sighed mournfully, while, all about, the leaves fell noiselessly to the ground.

But, of a sudden, the moaning of the wind in the tree-tops was changed to sweet music, and when the people looked aloft, they saw the branches clothed with bright green foliage. The myrtles and pomegranates had sprung out in full bloom and fragrance, and round about, the ground was covered with flowers, while the delicate white form of the dying girl lay suffused with rosy light.

At this moment her fair spirit took its flight, the chain about her ankles snapped asunder with a sound like the silvery peal of a bell, while the heavens that now lay wide open to the eyes of al' were filled with infinite splendor and majesty.

And there were seen thousands of fair boys and girls dancing in great circles in the white light of heaven. Now a glorious king, riding on a cloud on one border of which was stationed a royal choir of cherubs, descended towards the earth and received the sainted form of Musa before the eyes of all assembled in the garden.

The multitude continued to gaze until they saw her spring with a bound into the open heavens, where she was lost at once in the vibrant ranks of the shining dancers.

There was high holiday in heaven that day, and on holidays it was the custom (to be sure this is denied by Gregory of Nyssa, yet it is affirmed by Gregory of Nazianzus) to invite the nine Muses, who dwelt in Hades, into heaven, there to render assistance at the ceremonies. They were, on such occasions, dined sumptuously but were obliged, after having fulfilled their task, to return to the shades.

When on this day the dances and songs and all the ceremonies were over and the heavenly hosts were about to sit down to the feast, Musa was seated with the Nine Sisters, who sat nestling close together, casting shy glances hither and thither from the corners of their fiery black or tranquil dark-blue eyes. Martha, the industrious, mentioned in the gospels, was there to attend in person to their wants. She had donned her prettiest kitchen-apron, and the sweetest little spot of soot adorned her white chin. She was radiant, and insistently urged the Muses to help themselves to all the good things.

But not until Musa and Saint Cecilia and other women well versed in art-lore approached, and pleasantly greeting the shy Pierides, sat down with them, did they lay aside their shyness and appear at ease; but finally the intercourse among the fair banqueters became happy and free.

Musa sat next to Terpsichore; Cecilia sat between Polyhymnia and Euterpe, and all clasped one another's hands. Then came the cherubs, and seeking to ingratiate themselves by fond caresses, begged for some of the fruits that shone on the ambrosial board.

King David came also, holding in his hand a golden goblet from which each drank in turn. Joy animated the fair circle, as he walked complacently about the board, stopping a moment in passing to caress the cheek of the lovely Erato.

At the moment of supremest joy at the table of the Muses, Our Lady herself approached in all of her beauty and grace, and sat down for a little chat with them. When she at length departed she kissed high Urania tenderly upon the lips, whispering as she did so that she would never be content until the Muses were taken into Paradise forever.

But her wish was never realized, and this is the reason for it: To prove their gratitude for the kindnesses bestowed upon them and to show their good will, the Muses held a council and decided to prepare a song of praise to be given at their next appearance in heaven. The rehearsal was held in a remote spot of the Lower World, and they strove to imitate the form of the solemn choral songs customary in heaven. They formed two quartettes of their number, with Urania as a sort of leading voice for both. In this way they achieved a most remarkable vocal effect.

When at the next holiday in heaven the Muses were again invited to take part they took advantage of a moment which seemed timely, and assuming their respective places began gently to intonate their song, which soon rose and swelled mightily down the great corridors of heaven.

But alas! in these halls it sounded sombre and uncouth, indeed almost defiant, and so full of longing and sorrow was it that there fell upon the hearers a frightened silence. Gradually, as the song went on, all the folk of heaven were overcome by the burden of earth-woe and homesickness contained in it, and all burst into a torrent of tears.

A great sobbing was heard throughout the length and breadth of heaven, and all the elders and prophets rushed up astounded. But in their well-meaning zeal the Muses continued to sing louder and louder and in more melancholy strains than ever, and all Paradise with the patriarchs, elders, prophets, and all who had ever walked or reclined upon the green celestial meads were overcome by their emotions, and finally the Most High, approaching in person to right matters, silenced the Muses with a long-drawn peal of thunder.

Then quiet and peace were restored in heaven. But the unfortunate Nine Sisters were obliged to leave and have not again been invited to enter the sacred portals.